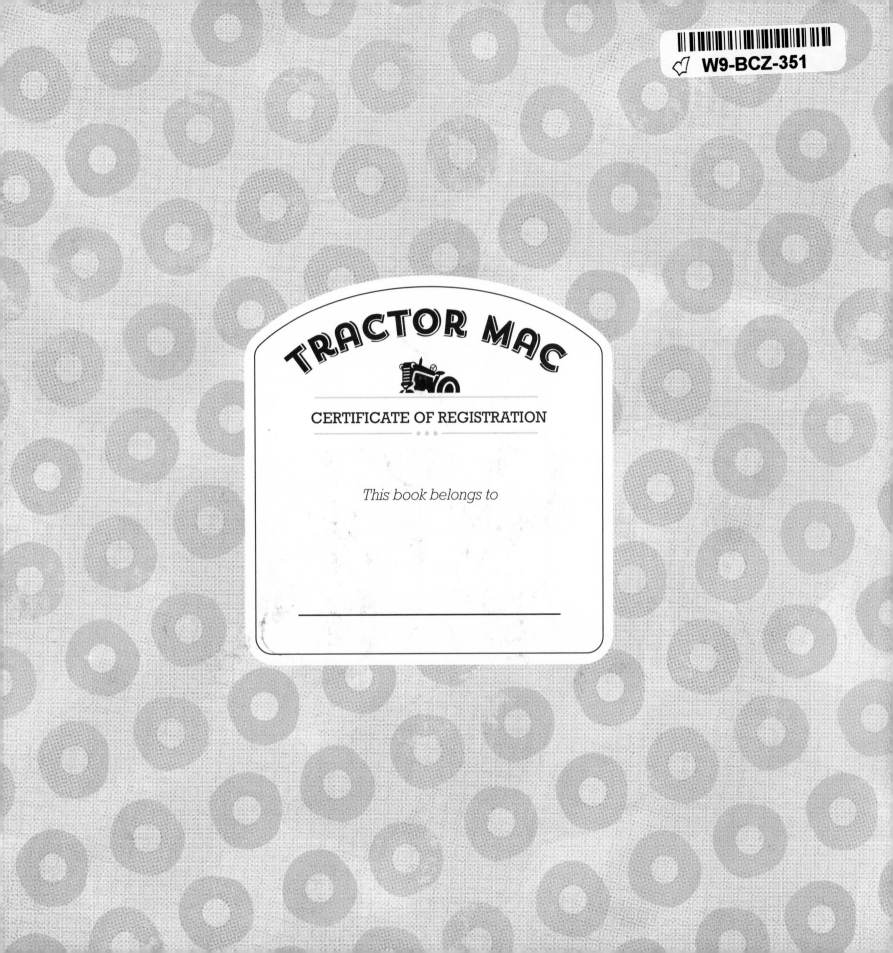

TRACTOR MAC

CERTIFICATE OF REGISTRATION

This book belongs to

_____

ALSO BY BILLY STEERS

TRACTOR MAC
SCHOOL DAY

Written and illustrated by
BILLY STEERS

FARRAR STRAUS GIROUX · NEW YORK

THE FIRST DAY OF SCHOOL WAS OVER. Betty the school bus was dropping off the last children on her route. "Oh dear!" she cried to Tractor Mac and his friends. "What a horrible day this has been."

"I missed some of my stops and got lost!" said Betty.

"I didn't even know how to use my signals properly."

"That does sound pretty bad," said Tucker Pickup. "I always stop when I see the signals flashing on a school bus."

"The other buses weren't very nice to me when I didn't know where to line up," said Betty sadly.

"Awfully abnormal," announced Bonnie the A bus.

"Bad blinkers," blurted Pat the B bus.

"Doubtful driving," declared Frank the D bus.

"I don't want to go back," sobbed Betty, honking her horn. "The children depend on you for a safe ride," said Sharon the sheep. "Without you, they won't be able to go to school."

"I'm scared that I will make the same mistakes again," said Betty.

"Listen," said Tractor Mac. "Ernie, the old school bus who used to drive this route, told me some of the tips he used. I think they will help you."

"Okay, Tractor Mac, I'm listening,"
said Betty. "But maybe I'd make a
better camper than school bus."

"Remember that sign in your window?" said Sharon. "You're the C bus."

"*C* is for cow!" mooed Margot the cow.

"The *C* is your clue," said Sibley.
"Ernie once told me that his bus route was shaped like the letter *C* drawn on a map," said Tractor Mac.

Tractor Mac made a big arc in the dirt with his tire. "You start in the valley where Carla is standing," he said, "then go up along the ridge and back down to the school, where I am."

"You'll learn your stops with practice," said Carla the chicken.

GRASSY TOP RD.

O.B. JOYFUL LN.

KRIS KROSS CT.

SCHOOLHOUSE RD.

FIRE TOWER

"Always use your safety flashers when you make a pickup," quacked Dudley the duck. "That way, the cars near you will know they should stop to let the children cross the street."

"I am a bus rider!" peeped a baby chick.

GOOD HILL RD.

STONY MEADOW FARM STAND

"Once school ends, keep in mind that you're the C bus," said Sibley.

"*C* is the third letter in the alphabet," added Sam the ram.

"So you line up as the third bus to pick up your kids," chimed in Goat Walter.

"That makes sense to me," said Betty.

"You can think of some words that begin with the letter *C* to keep you calm and competent on your route," said Tractor Mac.

"I'll try to be creative," said Betty. "I'm up to the challenge!"

"I know you can do it," said Tractor Mac. "You just need some practice! Why don't you try your route again this evening? Then you'll be ready for tomorrow morning."

As Betty practiced driving her C-shaped route, she tried to think of some C words.

She thought of *courage* and *character*.
To have courage means you're brave,
and Betty knew she was brave. And to have
character means you know how to do the right
thing even when it's not easy, and Betty knew she
could do that—she was doing it right now!

The next morning, Betty used her blinkers and stop sign each time she made a pickup. She smiled and was caring and cheerful for the children who rode her.

"I like this new school bus," she heard one little boy say.

At the end of the school day,
Betty got in third place, behind
two other buses.

"We have the best bus," said a
little girl.

"A-plus!" applauded Bonnie the A bus.

"Bravo, Betty," beeped Pat the B bus.

"Delighted to have you with us," decreed Frank the D bus.

When Betty made her last drop-off at the farm stand, she was happy.

"It looks like you had a better day!" clucked Carla the chicken.

"Three cheers for the cow bus!" called Margot.

"How different today was!" said Betty happily.

"If we make mistakes, it's proof that we're trying," said Tractor Mac. "That's how we learn."

"I agree with that!" grunted Paul the pig.

"Thank you all for helping me be confident!"
said Betty. "School is going to be fun."
"Certainly," said Tractor Mac.

To school bus drivers, who are entrusted to safely
transport children to school and back home

Farrar Straus Giroux Books for Young Readers
An imprint of Macmillan Publishing Group, LLC
175 Fifth Avenue, New York, NY 10010

Copyright © 2018 by Billy Steers
All rights reserved
Color separations by Bright Arts (H.K.) Ltd.
Printed in China by RR Donnelley Asia Printing Solutions Ltd., Dongguan City, Guangdong Province
Designed by Christina Dacanay
First edition, 2018
1 3 5 7 9 10 8 6 4 2

mackids.com

Library of Congress Cataloging-in-Publication Data

Names: Steers, Billy, author, illustrator.
Title: Tractor Mac school day / Billy Steers.
Description: First edition. | New York : Farrar Straus Giroux, 2018. |
Summary: Betty the school bus is upset over making mistakes on her very
first day, but Tractor Mac and the farm animals provide tips and encourage
her to practice and try again.
Identifiers: LCCN 2017042321 | ISBN 9780374306359 (hardcover)
Subjects: | CYAC: School buses—Fiction. | First day of school—Fiction. |
Perseverance (Ethics)—Fiction. | Tractors—Fiction. | Domestic
animals—Fiction.
Classification: LCC PZ7.S81536 Tqw 2018 | DDC [E]—dc23
LC record available at https://lccn.loc.gov/2017042321

Our books may be purchased in bulk for promotional, educational, or business use.
Please contact your local bookseller or the Macmillan Corporate and Premium Sales Department at
(800) 221-7945 ext. 5442 or by e-mail at MacmillanSpecialMarkets@macmillan.com.

ABOUT THE AUTHOR

Billy Steers is an author, illustrator, and commercial pilot. In addition to the Tractor Mac series, he has worked on forty other children's books. Mr. Steers raised horses and sheep on the farm where he grew up in Connecticut. Married with three sons, he still lives in Connecticut. Learn more about the Tractor Mac books at www.tractormac.com.